KINGPIN'S BABY

EVIE ROSE

Copyright © 2024 by Evie Rose

All rights reserved.

No part of this book may be reproduced in any form or by any electronic or mechanical means, including information storage and retrieval systems, without written permission from the author, except for the use of brief quotations in a book review.

This story is a work of fiction. Names, characters, places, and incidents are the product of the author's imagination or are used fictitiously. Any resemblance to actual events, locales, or persons, living or dead, is coincidental.

Cover: © 2024 by Evie Rose

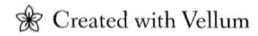

❋ Created with Vellum

ABOUT

I beg the Kingpin for help… He demands marriage in return.

Desperate, I ask my boss—the kingpin whose office I clean every morning while he works—to save me from a rival mafia who want money or they'll reveal all my secrets.
My boss is intimidating. Twice my age, a silver fox in a sharp black suit. But over the last year we've talked, the only people in the building as the sun rises, pink over the London skyline.

I'm shocked when he offers me a marriage of convenience.
A whirlwind wedding, and we promise it's just for show. No feelings. No love. A fake.
If anyone suspects my cover will be blown…
I know this has to be as close to a real marriage as

possible. If I can't have my husband's love, I will give him my V-card in one night together. And in exchange, I will have a sweet memory afterwards.

His baby.

Kingpin's Baby is a sweet and spicy age gap instalove romance with a jealous and possessive mafia boss billionaire hero and the girl he's been stalking.

1

REN

Every day my boss and I play death or donuts. At least, I think it's a game. Mr Booth is the kingpin of Fulham, the oldest and deadliest mafia in London. They're known for making awkward problems disappear. Permanently.

So perhaps he takes it more literally than I do?

I'm about to find out if a year of us debating the merits of donuts over the dubious choice of unaliving has made any difference to his murderous tendencies. Because today, the story I'll tell him is about *me*.

I hesitate at his door, butterflies taking flight in my stomach as they always do when I'm about to see Mr Booth. You'd think I would be used to his intense stares, dark scowls, and dry humour. But nope, I still get all fluttery.

Every. Morning.

It's naive and silly, but I adore my boss, and I'm just his cleaner, here in my sneakers and leggings at five in the morning. It doesn't hurt that he's gorgeous. A silver fox.

Black hair with flecks of grey, and deep green eyes that I lose myself in each time I look at him.

He always wears a black suit and a white shirt, everything understated but of the highest quality. He's classic and refined, just like this mansion that serves as his headquarters.

Direct gaze. Broad shoulders that I imagine I see everywhere. Ridiculous. There's a biker outside my apartment most evenings, wearing black leathers trimmed with green. I think he must be a courier or something. I spy on him through the curtains as he waits, sometimes tapping on his phone. I watch him, darkened visor down, and I have to remind myself that he can't be Mr Booth.

I kinda wish he was.

But what I really appreciate is the way Mr Booth listens, and seeks out my opinion. He doesn't always agree with it, I can tell, but he'll nod and though his mouth will twist with displeasure, he'll rumble that I have a point.

That considered agreement has made other opinions threaten to bubble up over the last few months. Words like, *I'd love to have your babies*, and *would you take my V-card?*

I think he'd be a perfect father. Gruff and kind and protective. And, I admit, part of my thoughts are most definitely about the fantasy of how he'd feel inside me. How it would be if he were on top of me, focusing all that scorchingly intense attention on my body.

Almost every day I bite my lip to prevent myself from saying things that would ruin it all. Powerful billionaire kingpins aren't interested in their cleaners. And they don't ride sleek black motorbikes.

My boss is as far from obtainable for me as flying to the moon.

Today, though, I'm extra nervous, in addition to concern about what I might say if I don't hold it in. Because I'm going to beg him to help me, and pray he's in a generous mood.

More donuts than death.

Taking a deep, steadying breath, I exhale, and open the door, looking in with a bright smile, as though this is a normal day and I'll repeat a story from the internet that has nothing to do with me. As if I haven't got my whole life on the line.

Mr Booth stares right at me. Waiting. His face is thunder, green eyes an impenetrable jungle full of poisonous snakes.

Oh. Sugar.

---

12 MONTHS EARLIER

People say that they'll die if they mess up their job, and sure, if you're a Navy SEAL or something, that's true.

Not usually the literal case for a cleaner, though.

The warnings of the kingpin's second-in-command echo through my mind.

Do not talk to Mr Booth.

Do not annoy Mr Booth.
Do not vacuum clean in the same room as Mr Booth.
Do not touch anything on Mr Booth's desk.
Do not ask what happened to the previous cleaner.

Those last two? Very important. Mr Harvey emphasised them several times.

But even murdery mafia bosses need their fancy Victorian mansion offices cleaned, and I need a job, so here I am, at the crack of dawn.

Five AM is an hour no one should see. Having been let in by a surly guard, I'm going to do all my work before anyone else is out of bed. I huff up two flights of stairs, my sleepy thigh muscles creaking in protest, and decide I'll start with Mr Booth's personal office. That's the safest option. Then I can be finishing off the communal spaces downstairs by the time he appears.

I breeze in, duster in hand, dragging my trusty red vacuum cleaner behind me, and grope around in the dark before dawn for the light switch.

It hardly illuminates anything when I find it, but it's enough. The room is an old-fashioned library, with walls of leather-bound books, a plush carpet you could use as a mattress, and the windows are black with spots of orange-gold. London. There's a heavy dark wood desk covered with papers, several expensive shiny devices, and a glowing computer screen shedding light onto the back of a massive chair that faces towards the window.

I pause and admire all this luxury. The view of London. The scent of wax polish and something smoky and *masculine*.

Oof.

I'm a tragic case. I googled Mr Booth, and let me tell you, my tummy got butterflies, but not from fear. Even in a photo, he exudes power and authority. In his office, it's almost as though I can feel his presence, perhaps because it has a vibe that is both intimidating and also reassuring and comfortable. Like being friends with a black bear. Terrifying, and yet soft and cuddly.

I begin with the dusting, in the corner, humming to myself as I make my way around. I know everyone says cleaning is the worst, but I really like it. There's nothing as good as making a room shiny and sweet smelling.

This opinion, I admit, may be due to lack of experience. I've always been the gawky shy girl with her nose in a book, so there are certain activities I concede most people believe are better than cleaning. But I've never done them, and I get a glow of pride from a room that is neat and sparkly.

The back of my neck prickles as I work. I rub it, but the hairs won't go down.

Maybe this old house is haunted? Perhaps that was what happened to the last cleaner? Saw a ghost and ran off. Or was dragged off by the apparition. Ugh, I have an overactive imagination. I blink at the books, the gold reflecting the light of the room. And that's when I see it.

Something reflected in the shine. It's not a shape so much as... I don't know. A movement behind me.

It's nothing. It has to be nothing.

But I turn all the same.

And in the leather chair at the desk, sits Mr Booth.

He's even more intimidating and gorgeous in real life. Black stubble covers his cheeks, and his dark hair is messed up, as though he's been running his hands through it. He has a square jaw and moss-green eyes. And he's watching me, a scowl on his face.

Do not annoy Mr Booth.

Well, that was a fail, wasn't it?

"I'm sorry," I whisper, and he continues to regard me, brows lowered.

I'm too young to die. I haven't lost my V-card. I haven't been in love. I haven't rubbed myself all over Mr Booth like a demented cat.

Really shouldn't do that last one. But I want to. He's in a white shirt with a black tie and gold cufflinks. And his hands, oh wow his hands. They're big and square and look like they would cover my entire torso. He wears an expensive gleaming watch and has the lightest dusting of hair on his wrists.

"We haven't met, Miss…"

"Smith." But that sounds formal. Not like me at all. "Renee Smith. My first foster parents were English, but I was found on a little boat the authorities thought came from France, so they called me Renee. But people call me Ren."

As I speak, I wring my duster in my hands and Mr Booth trails his gaze down my body—clad in leggings and an old hoody. My skin tingles even as I talk about my name like a doofus. As though he would be interested in me.

"I didn't think anyone would be here." Oh god I wish

I could shut up, but I haven't actually said the one thing that could save me. "I'm the new cleaner."

I clamp my mouth closed.

A trace of amusement lights Mr Booth's eyes so briefly I'm not certain it was ever there. "I see."

Do not talk to Mr Booth.

Crapola. Good job, Ren.

"I'll go."

But before I can turn and sprint out, a single word stops me.

"No."

I'm shaking, heart pounding, when I look back at Mr Booth. I bite my lip to stop myself from begging. Probably not to kill me, but I'm not sure I wouldn't like to be laid on that messy desk of his and spanked. Ravaged. Kissed. All of the above.

"It's fine," he says in a voice that's low and rough and like warm silk and whisky. "Please carry on, Miss Smith. Don't allow my insomnia to inconvenience you. One of us is quite enough, on that count."

With a jerky nod, I return to dusting the bookshelves. Behind me, there is the whoosh as he swivels his chair, then the soft sound of shuffled papers.

It takes a few minutes, but I'm working, and so is he. The silence and the gentle sounds of cloth on wood and pen to paper are soothing somehow. Against all the odds, the muscles on each side of my spine unclench.

It's perfectly domestic.

Ting!

I freeze.

"Your boyfriend texting you?" Mr Booth drawls in a dangerously soft voice.

"No!" I yelp, snatching my phone from my hoody pocket and poking it desperately to try to silence all messages. Hardly. "It's just a notification for a group I'm in."

Mr Booth raises one eyebrow.

"I don't have a boyfriend. The alert was from an internet site." That's even worse, isn't it? "An advice group," I babble. *Please don't kill me.* "People tell their story, and commenters say whether they are in the right, or what they deserve for what they did."

"Sounds like I'd be good at this," he replies dryly, and leans back in his big black leather chair. "Go on then. What's the question?"

Am I hallucinating?

I scan the post, taking it in.

"It's an office dispute. There's a group of work colleagues who team together and buy donuts every Friday."

I hazard a glance at Mr Booth, but his expression is scrupulously neutral.

"They leave them on the breakroom table until it's time for elevenses."

"Elevenses, being...?"

Mr Booth has never had elevenses? He's awake and at his desk at five in the morning, but isn't peckish by eleven. What is he, a machine? Pffs. Not even my phone can hold out until lunchtime. It needs to be plugged in by eleven or it dies.

"You know. Elevenses." I shrug. "A cup of tea and a snack at eleven o'clock."

"I see." His mouth twitches as though he might smile. He circles his hand, indicating for me to continue.

"Now there's a new guy at work, and he keeps eating the fancy glazed-with-sprinkles donuts for breakfast. At like, eight."

Mr Booth's expression has taken on a tint of exaggerated patience.

"A fight has broken out. The new dude has been told that the donuts are for elevenses, at *eleven*, but continues to eat them first thing in the morning. He says that donuts left out for a whole morning are fair game, and if they don't want anyone else to eat them, they shouldn't leave them on the breakroom table. The donut group say they like to anticipate their elevenses treat as they pass through the breakroom, and see what's been bought that week. And he should keep his hands to himself. Everyone else manages to restrain themselves. In response, he says... Well. It continues. That's the key bits."

There's a brief silence. My mouth goes dry.

Could really do with a cup of tea and a donut right now.

"What do you think?"

Mr Booth huffs. "I'd kill him."

"Seriously?" I burst out. "Overreaction, *much*?"

Two taps of his pen on the desk and Mr Booth narrows his green eyes.

"Sounds like he just gets hungry with that food around," I continue. I'm for the ride. Committed. "The boss needs to buy donuts, so there are enough for everyone, even if they want to eat it at the wrong time." Because elevenses is at eleven. That's the rule.

"Not death?" Mr Booth says sceptically.

"No, definitely not death. Donuts."

The corner of his mouth quirks up.

"Okay." He nods. "Donuts. What about this?"

He slides a sheet of paper across the desk towards me, and when I hesitate, gives a tiny nod.

It's a meticulously compiled report on the story, with ages, dates, all the facts of the case clearly laid out. It seems this man was one of Mr Booth's employees. It doesn't say what his role was, but my mind fills in cleaner. He was married to his childhood sweetheart, and was turning informant for the police. He was also cheating on his wife.

Before Fulham could deal with him, he met an untimely end at the hands of his vengeful wife. The report concludes that after adjustments to their records, the authorities believe the man has moved to Spain with an unnamed mistress. However, the disposing of the person who harmed a Fulham employee is pending Mr Booth's final decision.

I glance at his desk. It's littered with more neatly compiled reports.

"What do you think, Miss Smith?"

He makes decisions like this all day? It's complicated, and no one is innocent. She killed one of his men and even I know that mafias protect their own.

"Death or donuts?" He folds his arms and I'm drawn

again to notice how good-looking he is. His shirt is tailored but the lines of his muscles are clearly visible.

"Donuts."

I hold my breath, praying I made the right decision.

He makes a sound of dissent. "Why?"

Oh god. I got it wrong.

"She did you a favour. He was going to betray you to the police."

He nods slowly. "Fair point. He wouldn't have succeeded, since the police around here work for me. But I'll send her donuts along with my condolences, and best wishes for the future."

Then he stops attempting to hide the amusement twinkling in his eyes and I can't help but smile back. I somehow know that whatever I'd said, he would have listened and accepted my opinion as an equal.

"Thank you, Miss Smith."

I mustn't forget that he's a dangerous predator. A mafia boss.

"You're welcome, Mr Booth." I pull a cloth from my pocket and continue to dust the shelves, and our conversation is over. I resume my job, and he his. When I pause at the point I would usually use the vacuum cleaner, Mr Booth reads my mind, and says, "Go ahead."

Do not vacuum clean in the same room as Mr Booth.

The number of rules I'm breaking today isn't funny.

I do the whole floor and eventually I'm just creeping around close to his desk.

"I'm nearly finished," I assure him.

He rises gracefully and goes to stand at the window,

looking out on the white-pink and yellow London dawn. His hands in his pockets, his face in profile.

His expression is bleak. Lonely.

My heart tugs, reaching out to him. Like to like. Because how many times have I looked out from my bedroom window and felt as isolated as he appears right now.

This is a disaster.

I don't think he is going to kill me, but the trouble I'm in is much worse.

I fear I've just fallen in love with the billionaire mafia boss.

2

REN

Now

Mr Booth looks away, dismissively flicking some papers on his desk.

Since the first day, every time I walk into his office, Mr Booth looks up, spears me with those arsenic eyes of his, and asks, "What's today's death or donut question?"

But today, he doesn't. He picks up an expensive-looking pen and spins it agitatedly in his fingers.

I swallow.

"Mr Booth."

"Miss Smith." There's none of the usual warmth or dry wit in his tone.

This bodes wonderfully. My heart is beating so hard I suspect it will break several of my ribs by the time this conversation is over.

"Would you like to hear today's question?" My voice

breaks on the final word. He hasn't looked up. Why hasn't he looked up?

It's as though he knows I'm going to ask for his help and has already shut me out.

I think of the sinister, uniformed blond man who came to my apartment last night. I cannot fail.

Mr Booth doesn't reply. But slowly, oh so slowly, he raises his head and gazes right past me. It's so close, I doubt anyone else would notice that he wasn't looking into my eyes. But I've spent every morning with Mr Booth for months now, and I know what his regard does when it's on me. It tingles across my skin like animated liquid glitter.

And this, by contrast, is cold.

He flicks the pen onto the desk where it skims over the shiny wood, bounces against a stack of papers, then rolls to a stop.

His eyes are more shadowed than usual. As though he's tired. Maybe he didn't sleep well last night.

I probably look just as exhausted, and far worse, because I was up all night turning over this dilemma in my mind.

I wish I'd been with *him*.

"Yes."

Right. *Deep breath. No pressure, but you have one shot at this, Ren and if you fail, you'll never see the man you love again, possibly end up in prison, or maybe wind up... Yes. Well.*

"Twenty-two female, lives on her own. She's an orphan, and has lost contact with her foster families.

She's just minding her own business when one night, a man comes to her door."

Mr Booth is motionless, glaring at me. His pose, sitting back in his leather chair is deceptively casual. He's annoyed about something.

I almost want to ask him what's the matter, but he probably wouldn't tell me, as occasionally he shakes his head and says it's better if I don't know some mafia business details.

"He says he works for the Immigration Office, and also is involved with one of the London mafias. Then he says that she's being investigated, because she came to London as a baby illegally, brought by her now presumably deceased parents." I don't allow my voice to wobble. Much. "And does she have any documentation about her legal immigration status? It turns out, she doesn't. It seems when she got passed from foster home to foster home as a child, her paperwork got lost. So she's not eligible to remain in London. Her home."

Mr Booth's jaw tenses, but he doesn't say anything.

"The authorities are going to come after her, deport her. But the man offered her a way out. If she pays him a million pounds, he'll sort her citizenship. He tells her to steal it from her kingpin boss, and that if she tells him, he'll kill her."

Mr Booth goes very, very still.

"So." My lip trembles this time. "She's wondering what she should do. She can't steal the money because that will get her killed by her boss. If she tells her boss, the man might kill her. But maybe she could ask her boss to loan her the money, or to say to the authorities that her job can't be done by anyone else, so she gets a visa? She doesn't want to annoy her boss, but she's scared and doesn't want to be deported."

"Which mafia was that man from?" If possible, Mr Booth looks even angrier. The crease in his brow might go right down to his skull.

Wait, *that man*? Why has he phrased it that way rather than, *the* man?

Never mind.

"I don't know, he didn't say. I think that was intentional." My throat is drier than when I left dinner in the oven overnight then tried to eat it. "The man is returning tonight for his money. So, the question is: if she told her boss about what had happened, would that be death? Or donuts?"

He's completely motionless. Is he even breathing?

The silence drags out. It's so dense it's linking Mr Booth and me, and might consume us both.

"Death."

My chest crumples, the pain unspeakable.

"Or donuts," he continues, "is not the actual question here. Is it, Miss Smith?"

"No," I whisper. I'm trembling.

"Say it."

"I was hoping you could help. Please." I close my eyes as my voice breaks. Keeping my job would be perfect, and I'll beg for that. But I'm not too proud. If I can stay in London, that would be enough. Maybe I could walk past this office. Occasionally I'd glimpse him, from a distance.

That might keep my heart from utterly withering away for the lack of Mr Booth. "I need citizenship or money. I can't leave the country. Please, please help me."

"Miss Smith." His voice is dark and rough. "I'll help you."

Relief cascades through me, sudden and welcome as water in the desert. "Thank you so much. If you could just give me a statement that my job is—"

"You'll marry me."

3

JASPER

I really shouldn't be possessive of Renee. She isn't mine.

The anger that has consumed me overnight since I saw a man visiting her has been turned on whoever threatened her.

Nobody threatens Ren. Miss Smith. I should keep things formal between us. She's half my age, twice the beauty I deserve, and for all my wealth she instead has sweetness. I shouldn't be following her, or so protective. I have no claim over my innocent employee.

But she could be *my wife*.

"W-what?" Ren stammers.

"What you need is citizenship, yes? A marriage is the quickest way to achieve that." Also, as a significant bonus, she would have my name.

The jealous roar that has been in my head since I saw that man go into her apartment last night hasn't abated. Not even now I know that he wasn't invited, and wasn't her lover. No, that knowledge has just added a protective taint to my unrelenting need for her.

"You'll live here. With me." That will save me a lot of time spent idling outside her building on my motorcycle, or watching surveillance of her on my phone. "They won't take you from my house."

"Marriage?" Her brow furrows in confusion. "I thought you'd give me a fancier title of employment so they can't deport me? Chief senior executive... particulate matter removal... specialist."

I repress a smile. She's funny when she runs her mouth.

"Something that sounded important, but I could just continue with my current role," she adds.

"If that's what you prefer. How about, 'wife'?"

She gapes.

"Or do you think 'Mrs Booth' sounds better?"

I don't care which, or any name. The ball and chain. Her at home. Trouble and strife. My missus. I'll call her anything that means she doesn't leave my sight. The very thought is soothing my soul in a way I hadn't imagined possible. She's the key to my peace. For the last year, seeing her every morning and watching her has kept me going. Fed a growing obsession and need.

"You don't think they'd believe I was in a necessary employment?" she says, a bit forlorn, which I don't understand. As ever, she keeps talking, shifting from foot to foot nervously. "I know I'm just a cleaner, and nothing important, and you're kidding, about the wife thing, aren't you?"

There is so much wrong in that statement, it's a challenge to identify where to begin.

"I'm not joking, and those bastards are not getting donuts or a million pounds. They're getting death." There's shock in her face but I ignore it. She knows my business. I've told her day after day about the choices a mafia boss makes. "In the meantime, you need to not be deported. A contract of employment can be argued with. A marriage certificate can't."

"Yes, but—"

"Good, that's settled."

She blinks. "Marrying to give me citizenship?"

"Yes."

"Just... An in-name-only thing, right? A marriage of convenience." Ren scuffs the carpet with the toe of her sneaker. "No falling in love."

"Correct," I say, with honesty, even as my heart shrivels to a crisp. I'm not going to fall in love with her, I already have, the first moment she stepped into my office like a beeswax candle, small and warm and sweet-scented. I can't fall in love with her again.

I harboured secret, stupid hopes that this girl who is too good for me might grow to love me. But no.

She's as likely to want me as to spontaneously combust.

"Just temporary, I suppose, until this blows over. Were you thinking like, six months?"

"That's right." I force the words out. Half a year is more than I thought I'd ever get to possess Ren for. I should be grateful, not greedily wondering how I can have longer with her.

"And we wouldn't consummate the marriage," she checks, worry tugging at her eyebrows.

That's more difficult, because there's breathing, and there's breeding this girl, and I'm not sure which I'd choose if I had the opportunity. I can see the long-term advantages of oxygen, but if I could be inside her? See her pregnant by me? Hold our child in one arm and embrace her with the other?

Just once?

Worth it.

"I won't touch you. I promise."

Her nod is quick, and for the slightest split-second before she smiles, I kid myself there's sadness in her expression. "You'd really marry me so I can get citizenship? Why would you help me like that?"

Darling girl. She thinks I'm altruistic, when I'm being supremely selfish. She's given me an opportunity to own her, and keep her with me. Even without her skin on mine, being inside her, watching her come, or having her love, I'm as covetous as a dragon. I'll take ownership of her on paper if that's all I'll ever have.

If she was by my side, perhaps I'd be able to sleep?

See. Selfish.

My insomnia has become worse since we met. I'm restless when she's not here, impatient for her arrival. Plus, the temptation to look at the CCTV of her kitchen and check she's not awake is strong. I drew the line at surveillance in her bedroom, but if she was here in my house, as my wife...

I could watch her sleep.

"You want me to fix this? Marriage is the solution I'm offering." I can't tell her why. She's only twenty-two years old. If she knew her blood-stained older boss was obsessed with her, she'd take the deportation option.

"They won't believe us," Ren blurts out. "You? In love with me?" She tugs at her oversized T-shirt and scoffs. "No one is going to think it's real."

A baby. Instantly, that's the thought in my mind, unbidden. If she was pregnant with my child, as well as being my wife, there could be no doubt that our marriage was genuine. The fact that it would be true on my side, and a pretence on hers... Well. There's never a perfect solution. Grizzled old mafia bosses can buy the companionship, but not the love, of beautiful young women.

But that's not what she means. There are certain expectations around kingpin's wives. I reach into my desk drawer, and pluck out a matt black credit card that has a limit large enough to purchase London property. Sliding it towards her, I wish her affection could be bought as easily as pretty dresses.

"Use this to purchase anything you please."

She chokes and doesn't move to take it.

"Though, you don't have to change. I like you as you are."

"You do?" she replies faintly, gaze flicking between my face and the card, her expression one of suspicion, as if she's scared it might be a trap.

"Yes." If there was a London Mafia Syndicate annual award for understatements, I'm confident I'd win it with that answer.

"The man said he would return tonight, and that if I didn't have what he wanted, there would be men to deport me in the morning."

"You're staying here. No one is going to hurt you or take you from me."

"But you can't stop the authorities, if they have a legal—"

"No one. I'll dispose of anyone who tries to touch a hair on your head." My snarl is uncontrollable.

I've shocked her, I can tell. She recoils, fear in her eyes that's there and gone before I can fully analyse it.

Donuts. Right. My solution is always death, hers is donuts.

"Follow me." I stand abruptly, shove my chair away and stride to the door. With sheer effort, I don't look behind as I take the stairs up to my private apartments on the upper floors. By the time I've unlocked the door, Ren is beside me. I hold out the key, and Ren cups her palm under mine. As I tip it into her hand, I stroke my thumb over her wrist. It's a fast caress that I can't help, and her skin is velvet for that split-second touch.

Stolen. Deniable. I love her so damn much. I know I shouldn't, but I crave her.

"Make yourself at home," I say, my voice hoarse. "This is your place for as long as you're my fiancée, and then my wife."

She looks around, and I try to see the rooms through her eyes. Tidy. Plain. Perhaps a little empty.

We could fill it with kids...

I shake off the thought.

"There are a couple of bedrooms. Take whichever you want." I grind out those words.

"You think they'll believe it's a real marriage if we don't sleep in the same bedroom?" Ren spears me with her gaze, uncertain, and yet also... I wonder if she has any comprehension of how the tide of her blue eyes drags me around when she asks questions like that.

I could reassure her that there is an armed guard at every entrance. That I'll lock the entrance to this apartment and protect her with my life. No one will be asking about her sleeping arrangements.

"No." I point to my bedroom. Through the open door there's a peek of crisp white sheets and the palest of grey walls. "Have any of the rooms for your hobbies or whatever you like to do. But you'll sleep next to me."

She nods rapidly.

"We'll be married today. I'll get Harvey to hack into the registry so there's no delay. A wedding boutique will bring dresses for you to choose from and a stylist will deliver you new clothes to your specifications. I'm not risking anyone going back to your apartment." Although Harvey and a team will be lying in wait to catch the man who threatened Ren, find out who he's working for, and dispose of him. Painfully.

"When I said no one would believe us," she interrupts me, shifting from foot to foot. "I meant that..."

"What?" I demand. I am very invested in this plan. Nothing will stand in the way.

"No one will think we're engaged because we've never even touched."

My head goes light. *To have and to hold.*

She'll allow me to hold her?

Only two nights ago I watched a grainy image of her making a cup of tea, and was satisfied with that much. Only last night I was sick with jealousy thinking she had a lover in the other room, furious with myself for not putting a camera in her bedroom.

And now I get to touch her?

"Yes."

She holds out a tentative hand, watching my reaction as she draws closer.

All I can do is stare down at her. This slight, willowy girl who I love with my whole black heart.

Her fingers grasp my lapel, and her pupils are blown as she tugs at me and boosts onto tiptoes.

She can't mean...

There are moments when you know what is going to happen, but your mind won't accept it. As though it's protecting itself, trying to find some other explanation, because the one all the signs indicate is too much to wish for. Because if you allow yourself to hope you can be disappointed.

I've never permitted myself even a scrap of hope where Ren is concerned, so this takes me by surprise.

She's going to kiss me. I know it, but the impossibility

makes me stupid. Her lips land on mine, or maybe mine go to hers.

It's as innocent and sweet as she is. A press of lips, but my body instantly stirs.

My cock throbs, hard and demanding. My hand goes to her hair without thinking. That smooth honey-and-butter-on-toast-coloured hair. I groan. It's even softer than I imagined. Like warm liquid silk.

She kisses me tentatively, with questioning brushes and breathy sighs. And I wonder as desire mounts in me, whether she has done this before. Could this be her first kiss? Is that possible?

She presses herself to me from thigh to the plushness of her breasts.

I allow my lips to open, and holding her head, I deepen the kiss, sliding my tongue into the heat of her waiting mouth.

She melts as I explore, slowly and softly. Her response isn't that of an experienced woman unleashed. No, it's the gentle awakening of the innocent I've always thought her. It's acceptance of everything I give, from teasing sweeps of my tongue to hungry drags of my lips on hers. Her hands find my waist and my arm, first in an uncertain touch, then clinging.

And I battle my instinct to push her onto the nearest bed and see how far she'll let me go. She started it. I'd have never asked for a kiss, I'm already pushing my luck, but I'm a bad man. Presented with Ren's sweet kiss of thanks and practice I'm kissing her thoroughly, like we might never do this again and I'm attempting to slowly work my way through every possible variation of our mouths together. I'm rock-hard, driving my fingers further into that ponytail and pulling her soft body against me.

I want her so badly. I have to get her naked and be inside her. There's far too much clothing between us.

That thought stops me, somehow, even as Ren rubs herself against me.

Too much clothing?

I ease back.

Too fast. She asked for help with those extortionists, nothing more. Swallowing my need, I release her and, for good measure, take a step away.

One kiss and all the thoughts I'd pushed down of breeding Ren, of my wife having a child, of the family I can imagine us having have popped back up. Cute and funny kids, a bit of chaos, Ren presiding over it all, keeping everyone in order. I'd never get any sleep, but why would I care about that if I had Ren, pregnant, beautiful, smiling?

Her glance is shy as she looks up at me through her lashes.

This perfect woman is going to be my wife.

"I'll sort the licence. Please purchase anything and everything you want for our wedding." Our wedding. I turn before I say something even more revealing. But I pause in the doorway. "Money is no object. I'll be in my office if you need me."

Then I'm tearing myself away from her, walking downstairs in a daze. While I want more than anything for her to have my baby, stand by my side, a balance to my darkness, I can't.

All I can do is keep her safe. From her blackmailers, by scrubbing those bastards preying on vulnerable people from the face of the earth. It's one thing extorting money from those who can afford it. But from someone like Ren? Revolting.

Trying to blackmail *Ren?* I will take bloody revenge against them for scaring her.

But Ren requires more protection. From me.

4

JASPER

I wouldn't have heard the knock if I'd actually been working. But I'm not. I'm thinking about my fiancée upstairs, planning our wedding.

"Mr Booth?" Ren whispers, not advancing into the room. "Is it alright if I come in?"

"You don't have to ask." My heart thuds louder than she knocked on the door. "And you should call me Jasper, since you're going to be my wife."

She slips in, closing the door behind her. Then it's just her and me, and no cleaning cloths. It's the same, but not at all. Because it's not five in the morning, and she's still here.

"Jasper," she whispers, her cheeks flushing pink.

I rise and indicate the sofa in the corner. Ren follows, taking the seat next to me, perching on the edge, shoulders hunched, but her body slants towards me like a flower opening in the sunshine, despite itself. I want to see her grow in confidence.

"I wanted to ask about some things for the wedding?"

"Harvey has arranged a church, correct?"

"Yes, and they need to know details as soon as possible." She sounds a bit panicky. "Number of guests—"

"Your friends? Or anyone you consider family? Do you want anyone with you?"

She pauses, then forces out a sad little chuckle. "No. Not really. All my friends are online. And my biological family are..."

"They didn't get donuts," I surmise dryly, and she chuffs a half-laugh. "Me too," I confess, and it's raw in a way it hasn't been for decades.

"I'm sorry." Ren places her hand onto my thigh in a gesture of comfort, then flushes and snatches it back as though burned. "What happened?"

"My father died when I was seventeen. It was messy." That's one way to say that I ended up disposing of all three of my cousins when they came for me after he died of a sudden heart attack. They underestimated how prepared I'd be, even at that age. "Have you chosen a dress?"

That tugs a nervous smile from her. "Yes. They're doing alterations, but it'll be ready. Want to see?" She pulls her phone from her pocket.

"Aren't I not supposed to see it before the wedding?" The last thing I need is bad luck. "What else?"

"We have to choose vows, and sort church decorations. I don't want to get it wrong..."

"You won't." I'd defend every decision she made.

"Okay, but what about this wording..." She attempts to show me on her tiny phone screen, and I roll my eyes.

"Ugh, print that out, then we can discuss it. Or summarise it." I like it when she does that in the mornings, bringing her wit and personality to the tales.

"Sorry, I forget that you're..." She pauses. "A little older than me, and have different preferences about reading."

"Experienced, princess," I correct her. We need to get back to her not remembering how old I am or how inappropriate it is for me to be marrying a woman half my age. "And I have impeccable taste."

That she barks a laugh at. "What are you doing marrying me then?"

My hand shoots out and I have her ponytail in my fist and her head tipped back before I've analysed whether terrifying my fiancée is a good idea.

"Don't insult my wife-to-be." My voice is low, husky, and furious. "I've killed men for less."

Her lips part and she freezes, like the soft little prey animal she is. Our gazes meet and there's a frisson in the air.

I want to kiss that attitude from her. Kiss her or smack her sweet arse until she agrees with me. She's a princess, I won't have anyone say otherwise. Not even her.

"Understand?"

"Yes," she whimpers.

Pain digs into my chest. I'm hurting her.

I release her hair and sit back.

"Now, be a good girl and print those documents so we can look at them together."

"Yes, Mr Booth," she replies, smoothing her T-shirt as she rises, her spine straighter, her head higher even as she figures out how to make the printer work. I catch a pleased smile as she gathers up the papers.

Huh. Maybe she wasn't hurt...

"They want details about music, too." She sits back down, closer this time, and our fingers touch as she passes me the printouts.

"What music would you like?"

Clasping her hands together, as though she's treasuring the place where we made contact as much as I did, she bites her lip. "Something traditional? Classic? But I don't know any of the names of the pieces, and I'm confused."

Side by side, her arm brushing mine when one of us indicates a phrase, or searches for a paper, we work through every decision on her list, and as we do, Ren's confidence blooms. It's so natural. Just like when we play death or donuts, we go back and forth about the details, serious and playful at the same time.

We're there for hours. Harvey brings lunch, and Ren nibbles the excellent sandwiches made by my chef. I've never had anyone to work *with*, apart from Ren. Harvey might be my second-in-command, but he wouldn't dare challenge me, shy but determined, like Ren does. The closest I've ever been to sharing my burdens is showing Ren the daily dilemmas. That person defaulting on their loan, this other selling secrets to Westminster.

She's young and unworldly, and I find it charming that when I suggest flowers, poems, or music she clearly doesn't know what I mean, and agrees, taking copious notes and asking me for the spellings of lisianthus and Mendelssohn.

I wonder what else would be new to her? I'd love to introduce her to all the best aspects of life...

My cock goes hard at the thought, and it takes everything in me to focus on what she's saying rather than speculate about whether I'd be the first to lick her sweet folds.

Look, I can control myself around her. More or less.

"There's a part here about rings..." Ren says tentatively. "What do you think?"

"I'll sort those."

"I don't want to inconvenience you," she protests.

"You're not." But there's something else, isn't there? "Hold on."

Ren gasps as the lowermost shelf of books behind my desk swings open to reveal the safe.

"That's so cool!"

I grin as I pull the flat leather case out. Another first for me.

"I'm not sure what's in here," I say as I settle back onto the sofa next to her, and she shuffles until her bare arm rustles my shirtsleeve. I've never had any impulse to think about engagement rings or shiny adornments. Until now.

The clasp is a bit stiff, but the lid pops open and Ren

gives a sigh as row upon row of rings and necklaces appear.

"Choose whatever you like, and consider it an engagement present." I like the idea of her wearing my ring.

"Why do you have all this jewellery?" She skims her forefinger over the gems.

"Fulham has been around for a while." I am loving my understatements today.

"Were these your mother's?"

My throat goes dry. "Probably. She disappeared when I was eleven. About the same time as the kingpin of Westminster's mother, incidentally."

"Wow. Do you think…?"

"I imagine they're happy, somewhere. Eating donuts." I hope so, anyway, and the sentiment makes Ren smile.

"Is this one too much? The square one?" She points at a big, but not the largest or showiest, ring, with a single inverted pyramid diamond set in yellow gold.

"Try it on."

She regards me from under her lashes as she fits the ring to her fourth finger then holds out her hand, turning it this way and that, admiring it.

"A princess cut diamond for my princess."

"It's a bit too big." The ring has a small gap. "I don't want to lose it."

"If you can cope for now, we'll adjust it for you." I wonder if she knows I'm not talking about the ring, but the role. Wife.

"Okay." She closes her other hand over it, as though keeping the ring on her finger. "I'll keep it safe." She takes a deep breath and then sighs. "That's all the wedding stuff." Reaching for the printouts, she shuffles them. "So I guess I'm going to go back upstairs, out of your way. Make calls. Sort out these things."

"Very well." It's no more than I expected that she wants to get away from me. But I have something like regret in my heart.

Perhaps she could plan a wedding for us every day, so she'd have to come and consult me on it. Or a baby is an even better option. She'd need advice about names, clothes, and a myriad of other things.

I keep my hands and thoughts to myself as I settle back behind my desk. She's right, there's work to do. At the door, Ren stops, fiddling with her new and unfamiliar ring.

I wait.

"I was thinking about us appearing natural." She doesn't look at me. "And I was wondering..."

"Go on."

"Most couples have been..." she hesitates, twisting her legs, pressing her thighs together. "*Intimate* by the time they get married."

"I see." I can't breathe. "What were you thinking? Another kiss?"

She bites her lip and nods, but her eyes speak for her. Disappointment.

Oh, not just another kiss then.

Sliding my chair away from the desk, I lean back and

observe her. So pretty. My future wife is all curves and fine lines with her pale hair and soft blue eyes. The colour of the stormy sea.

"You don't need to do this." I force the words out.

"I know." She ducks her head and squirms. "But I wouldn't want anyone to think this wasn't real." Then I see it. She's shifting, hips undulating, continuously trying to get contact on her clit.

Something has turned her on, and she needs to come.

I won't take advantage. She said she didn't want a real marriage, so I'll adhere to the letter of the law she set when she was in a clearer frame of mind.

My elbow on the armrest, I beckon her with one finger.

A sigh of relief and she almost skips to me. I suppress a smile. There's no guile about my fiancée. No sultry artfulness in swinging her hips or wearing revealing clothing. She's as fresh and sweet and honest as a daisy.

"Sit on the desk," I command when she reaches me.

There's no hesitation. She plunks her cute arse onto the edge of the wood, and places the pile of notes to the side. She's so petite that she doesn't disturb the chaos of paperwork behind her, and gazes at me like I'm her personal saviour.

I go to remove her leggings, but before I touch her, remember my manners. Hell. Ren makes me forget myself.

"May I?"

She licks her lips and gives a quick nod.

Sliding my hands underneath her T-shirt, I find the

waistband. My thumb touches a sliver of skin. She trembles as I stroke her, then hook the elastic, and drag it down, taking her knickers too. But she lifts her bottom to allow me to roll the fabric down her thighs and reveal her, even toeing off her shoes as I get the leggings to her ankles.

"Mmm, I quite like the idea of you held," I murmur, hardly for her ears, as I release her feet and toss the garments away.

But she hears, and when I look up, she's blushing prettily.

"Pull up your T-shirt for me, princess."

Her obedience is unexpected and dizzying. There's no argument. She just grasps the hem of her T-shirt and tugs it right over her head and drops it onto the floor.

"Like that?"

"Yes." One hoarse word is all I can get out. She's stunning, and not been wearing a bra, all this time. She's been so close to naked while I've been in layer after layer of suit. Her tits are the finest artwork I've ever seen, her skin smooth and enticing.

Watching her eyes, I lean in and kiss her belly. It's a silent promise. I'll put a baby in there, sooner or later.

One thing is for certain. I won't let her go.

Everything I said about this marriage only lasting six months? A lie. I won't stop her leaving.

But I have six months to turn this from a deal to her enthusiastically bouncing on my cock. I'll just make it so she doesn't want to go. I'll give her orgasm after orgasm. I'll tell her off if her credit card bill isn't high enough.

Hell, I'll start going to the godforsaken do-gooder London Mafia Syndicate meetings so she can make friends with the other mafia wives. Literally anything. I'll do all I can to make her happy. Deliriously happy, so she stays with me.

Not just so I can sleep. Yes, she calms the beast inside me.

Working my way down from her belly button, her breathing goes ragged as I hold her hips and pretend her soft stomach is all I'm interested in. But there's an end I have in mind here, and when I glance up, I find her expression full of trust and awe.

I can't restrain my grin.

"Open your legs, princess."

Tentatively, she parts her knees, revealing her pink folds. They're soaked.

My cock surges.

"You look delicious." I begin slowly, with kisses over her thighs. Gentle presses of my lips onto her soft flesh. Yielding and so lovely.

I draw slightly closer with every kiss, and the anticipation makes my heart pound. I lure her in, pretending this is all I'm interested in. I indulge in teasing touches, not quite where she needs it. Her juices already coat my mouth, and her taste? Oh she tastes amazing. A bit sweet, a bit salty, and entirely of Ren.

Her gasp of surprise turns into a moan as I reach her clit with short, light licks that explore. Then firmer, more. I circle my tongue over the sensitive bud again and again, and she writhes and whimpers.

I have to feel her.

Keeping one hand on her thigh, I bring the other to her entrance. There's no need to moisten my fingers. Between her arousal and my licks, she's soaked.

I touch a fingertip to her where she yields, and continue to suck and lave her clit. I'm waiting for her to move away, or say no, or point out that we shouldn't do this. I'm twice her age. I'm her boss. I'm a kingpin and she's in a vulnerable position.

She doesn't say any of those things.

Nope.

She begs. "Please." And spreads her legs wider for me.

I slide my forefinger into her tight wet heat, and groan, even as I continue to lick her. My cock is seeping pre-come from the second-hand pleasure. Withdrawing, I push in again, deeper, and she whimpers, shifting her hips towards me.

All the time, we're watching each other. And after months of this being one-sided, of observing her alone, her eyes on me as I feast is a special kind of caress. I don't need her hands on my cock, I have her gaze.

"I love this pussy," I tell her, and scrape my teeth over her clit, biting gently at the tender bud. She jerks, and cruel man that I am, I laugh before I return to licking her. Harder this time, more insistent. I want to feel her quake underneath me.

Then I go after her orgasm with determination.

She whines softly, head thrown back, propping herself up on her hands. "Jasper."

I ignore the ache of my jaw and the cramping of my tongue and alternate between sucking her and hard swipes to and fro over her clit, and stroke her from the inside out. One finger, then I add a second and damn but she's tight and hot and perfect.

"Come for me," I demand.

As I thrust a third finger into her, she breaks, shuddering and grasping my fingers in her pussy as she comes in pulse after pulse. Her moans are so loud they must be able to hear her right through the building, despite the old stone walls.

I've never heard anything more beautiful. Honestly, should have recorded that, I'd have it on loop.

In fact...

"That was very good, princess." I look up from between her legs. My cock is so hard it hurts, a metal pole digging into my belly but also throbbing with desire that won't be satisfied.

I want to push myself inside her and take. Obviously I do.

But for now, it's another need that I'll sate. Pleasuring my girl until she's wiped out.

Gathering her into my arms, she rests her head on my chest as I carry her to the large sofa we were sitting on earlier.

She remains curled there for long minutes, and I stroke her hair and delight in her small, curvy body in my lap.

"What now?" she says eventually, attempting to move.

This is what I've been waiting for. I shift and sprawl back across the cushions, leaving her upright, surprise pinching her face.

Grabbing her arse, I tug her up over my chest, until she's naked, sitting on my collarbones, knees over my shoulders. I urge her further forwards, onto my mouth. She resists.

"Jasper! How will you breathe?"

I shrug happily. "If I die, I die. It's the price of donuts."

"You're insane."

I bend my neck up and give her a long, leisurely lick. She bucks, almost crying, and I smile. "What better way is there for us to be sure that we trust each other? As you said, to be convincing we need to have been close. What could be more intimate?"

She opens her mouth and obviously considers whether to say sex. And yeah, I'm up for that too. Literally. And there are many other things I'd like to do. But the hours while she chose a wedding dress, and we decided how our wedding would proceed, have clarified a few principles for me.

When I claim her, I want to breed her. I've waited and denied myself this long, saying that she's too young for me and too innocent to be involved with me. I'll take this.

"Now, princess. Again."

5

REN

This dress is excessive. It's pure white silk, with a swooping neckline and just the right amount of decoration. When I looked at it on the rack, there was a similar sense of recognition as when I first saw Mr Booth.

As I smooth my hands over the skirt, I feel like a fairytale princess. A very nervous one. Maybe I could be in a cute holiday movie? And while I'd hesitate to say Mr Booth is Prince Charming, I'm certain I'm marrying the love of my life.

I stand at the door to the church as the sun sets pink and orange and lilac behind me. Somehow, I'm even more anxious than I was when I was about to ask for Mr Booth's help, just twelve hours ago.

Then the risk was only that I'd lose everything. Now, I could lose something more difficult to replace: hope.

Jasper insisted we do this properly. I arrived on my own in a white limo I'm pretty certain was armour plated —with six of his men as bodyguards—and he's already inside. At least, I hope he is. If Jasper isn't in the church, I'm probably going to bawl my eyes out like a bride in a rom-com movie.

"Ready?" Harvey asks, eying me as though concerned I might run, and what his boss would do to him if I did.

This is insane. But I'm going to marry Mr Booth, and try to squeeze every bit of happiness I can from our fake marriage.

I nod to Harvey and the heavy old wooden double doors swing open before me.

I gasp. The church is in shadow, lit with hundreds of white candles, draped with garlands of flowers, and the path to the altar is strewn with rose petals.

It's magical.

Mr Booth stands alone, the conductor of all of this, in his customary perfectly fitted black suit and dark tie. He's staring right at the door, at *me*, his hands in his pockets and his expression arrogant. Uncaring.

His jaw scruffier than I've ever seen it first thing in the morning, and I see a flash of relief in his pinewood eyes when he sees me. Organ music swells, and I take the first step towards Mr Booth without thinking, on pure instinct.

My dress sweeps on the petals as I walk slowly, as though compelled by his will and the surroundings.

"Princess," he breathes, taking my hand and drawing me to stand at the front of the church, sweeping his gaze over me, from head to toe.

Things happen like I'm in a dream. Harvey takes my bouquet, Jasper and I turn together towards the altar, the priest says words. There are answers about free will and our names. Jasper's upper arm brushes my shoulder, solid and reassuring. But I can't stop sneaking glances at my future husband, and each time, he senses my eyes on him, and our gazes meet.

It's as though there's a bubble around and connecting us.

I say my vows in a daze.

"To have and to hold." His voice rumbles through me. "...Love and cherish..."

I could cry with how much I want all this to be real.

Jasper's expression is serious as he repeats the words, brows low, no hint of a smile.

He's hating this, isn't he?

I should have asked for a loan, and not told him the whole story. That would hurt less, surely? Or perhaps I ought to have insisted we wait and planned a bigger wedding. People, fuss. If it weren't just the two of us and a priest and his men, we could excuse Jasper's sombre mood on something other than that he's marrying me because he felt bad for his little cleaner.

Ugh. I'm an idiot. Because despite all that, this is the most special moment of my life.

"And the exchange of rings," the priest says.

"Exchange?" I blurt out before I can censor myself.

I know lots of men don't wear wedding rings. I never imagined that Mr Booth would, especially not since this is all for show.

"Yes, princess. I belong to you as much as you belong to me," Jasper replies with casual patience, as though that's the sort of thing he repeats to me three times a day.

He belongs to *me?* This wild panther of a man is mine? It sends the best shiver down my spine before I remind myself that he's *so* good at faking.

Mr Booth doesn't need to do so much as raise his hand an inch, and Harvey is at his elbow. Plucking a ring from the pillow, my nearly-husband takes my hands in his, ignoring the priest altogether.

It's a plain gold band. Classic, simple. I have a moment's apprehension that it won't fit, after all we didn't discuss this. The gold is cool as he slips it over the tip of my finger.

"I give you this ring," he murmurs as he slides the glinting band over my knuckle and into place, seated on my finger. "As a sign of my love."

The words flow through me, warm and caressing. As a sign of *his love*. I know this is just a favour, a marriage of convenience. But my body responds as though it's true—a lump in my throat and happy tears threatening behind my eyes—because he sounds like he means it.

The ring fits, perfectly snug.

I look up into his face and find my boss smiling down at me and what was a tender moment of pretend becomes sweeter and more bitter simultaneously. Because he is the best actor in London. No one could possibly see his expression and not believe he was in love.

Except me.

He strokes his thumb possessively over my fingers, lingering on the gold band. The silence draws out as we do nothing but stand there, gazing at each other, my hand in his. My heart is his too.

"Very good," the priest says softly. "And Miss Smith?"

The pillow with his ring is there, and Jasper doesn't release my fingers, still stroking firmly but slowly, with what feels like possessive instinct.

My hand slides over his and his grip tightens for a split-second before he lets me go and offers his fingers.

"I give you this ring as a sign of my love." I try not to think about how one-sided this is. All the advantages for me, all the risk and prosperity on his side...

Wait, what about a prenup? This is a marriage of convenience, he was very clear about that. But when we split up, Jasper will forfeit half his very considerable wealth.

He's a *billionaire*. My head spins.

"Now, to sign the register. This way, please." The priest's eyes twinkle behind his thin-framed glasses.

"What about a prenup?" I hiss as we follow, darting my gaze to the side, hoping the priest and his assistant won't hear.

"No need." Jasper's fingers tighten on my arm, but his voice remains unruffled. He hurries us after the priest, into a little antechamber where there's a small table with a book lying open. He sits me into the single chair.

"But—" I protest quietly. He isn't protected at all. I'm so stupid, how could I have done this? I don't want Jasper to suffer for helping me.

"I said, no need," Jasper repeats, soft but uncompromising. "You are not backing out now. Sign, princess."

Is he worried I'm not going to marry him? I flick my gaze to his eyes, and they're steel.

I pick up the pen. I don't care about the money, or even the citizenship that started all this. I love *him*. If I just need to trust him? Okay. I do.

My boss' hand holding the page, I write my name—I still don't have a proper signature, what is one supposed to be?—as Jasper looms over me. This is official, and we're faking, and while when we said the words at the front of the church it felt romantic and exciting, this feels... I don't know. Heart-thumpingly confusing. Because why didn't he want a prenup?

And why did he seem upset that he thought I might back out?

No sooner than I've lifted the pen from the paper, Mr Booth plucks it from my fingers, scrawls an elegant but illegible signature next to his name, tosses the pen aside and pulls me to my feet.

Then he lets out a deep sigh, as though he'd been holding his breath and drags his gaze proprietarily down my body.

"Wife." And though it's a low rumble, there's a smile in his eyes.

"Ah-hum." The priest clears his throat. "The rest of the ceremony, Mr Booth."

My boss grabs my hand and leads me back to our place amongst the flowers and candles in the church.

He doesn't even bother to turn us to look at the priest, his green eyes dark in the shadowed light.

"I now pronounce you, man and wife. You may kiss the bride."

My heart rate kicks up as Jasper tips up my chin with one hand and slides the other around my waist to draw me to him with such tenderness I can barely cope.

"Mine," he whispers so quietly I think I've imagined it before our lips touch and every rational thought flies. He kisses me like it's his right, which I suppose it is. I'm putty in his hands. We're doing an excellent impression of a couple so in love that we can't restrain ourselves when he glides his hand to hold the exposed nape of my neck.

In part because fifty per cent of us are.

He kisses me with equal intensity to earlier, pressing our bodies together. He's hard where I'm soft, and the contrast steals my breath away. When he withdraws, I'm left panting and flushed. Jasper smiles slowly while I'm still mush.

"Come on, princess." Lacing his big fingers with my smaller ones, we walk back down the aisle to the clapping of his men, and more music of the type that epic moments running across fields are made to in movies.

And I begin to think that spectacular as our wedding has been, this isn't what I've been anticipating.

No. What I'm looking forward to is tonight. Once I'm in my fake husband's bed.

As his wife.

Then we step out of the church, and at the bottom of the steps is a familiar motorcycle.

6

JASPER

The statement, "I love my wife" ought not to surprise anyone, least of all said wife.

But I promised her a marriage of convenience. Six months. No love, no lust, no over-the-top displays of possessive rage. Just protection and a passport.

It's not her problem that the past eighteen hours have been the happiest of my life.

The last five minutes, when the priest announced she was my *wife*? The very best.

So of course now I realise I've possibly spoiled everything.

"Mr Booth." She licks her lips and stares. "Jasper..."

"If you're looking for more names for me, you can try, husband."

She turns, sliding her hand from mine. "How about, stalker?"

I briefly consider denial, but instead shove my hands in my pockets. "You noticed."

It's too late, I remind myself. We're married. She can't run away from me now.

"It was you."

I incline my head in what could be a nod, or hanging in shame. I'm not sure which it is.

"I recognise your..." She gestures. "Bike."

"There aren't many Arch motorcycles around," I concede. Particularly not since it's a custom-made jasper-stone-green and matt black bike that cost more than most London houses. "Come on." I grab her hand and she follows me down the church steps.

"Are you sure this is a good idea?" she asks, a tremor in her voice as Harvey appears at my elbow with our leathers and helmets.

In answer, I take from Harvey the jacket I presumptuously bought for her the morning after we first met. Despite her protest, she allows me to slide her arms into it and shrug it on.

"Why do you want to do this? Why not the car?"

I zip the black leather jacket slowly up to her chin, then look into her uncertain eyes. Those soft blue eyes will be the death of me.

"Because the only time I'm free is when I'm riding this bike. Or I'm with you."

Her mouth falls open.

I hold out my hand for her helmet, and when I pause with it above her head—at my eye level, damn but she's tiny—she nods. And my heart expands as I lower the sleek, top-of-the-range protection down to cover her face. Because just as I hoped, she understands.

The only time I leave all the cares of being a kingpin behind is when I drive through London anonymously on this bike, and idle outside her apartment, keeping watch.

It's the work of a moment to shrug on my leathers, nod to my second-in-command, and lift Ren onto the seat, tucking her skirt closely and safely under her legs. I don't allow myself to linger, throwing my leg over the bike in front of her.

"Wrap your arms around my waist, hold on, and move with me," I murmur, and she squeaks with surprise. "Radio link in the helmets," I explain with a chuckle.

The roar of the engine doubles the peace I feel from her grip on my ribcage. She's holding tight. For a long time this bike has been my one indulgence, a slice of normality—sort of—in a life of brutal privilege and responsibility. There are no complicated decisions to make, it's all instinctive. A thrill to push myself and the machine.

And as I accelerate into the ink and gold London street, with Ren at my back, my head clears. This is where I'm supposed to be. With her.

"Oh my god!" Ren squeals and then disintegrates into delighted giggles, hugging me as I go faster. "It's like flying!"

She's a natural, leaning with me into every turn as we speed through the quiet of the nighttime roads.

"Jasper, can I ask you something?" she says after her laughter has faded away and a few minutes have passed.

"Yes," I reply promptly, though I know this conversation has the potential to break everything.

"Why did you hang around outside my apartment building?"

"Same reason as I had a hidden camera in your kitchen."

Her sharp intake of breath stabs down into my left pectoral, right to my heart. She's my wife now. She can't leave me.

I tell myself that, but I know it's a lie. The silence between us stretches out, even though the engine should block all sound.

"And why was that?" she asks eventually.

I can't bring myself to spoil our wedding day with my obsessive love for her. I can't bear that she'd pull away. Not yet. I raise my shoulders the smallest amount. "Why do you think?"

"I don't know."

"To protect you." That's enough, isn't it? Plausible for a mafia boss. I allow her to imagine that I treat all my employees to this level of scrutiny and care.

The journey isn't far, and all too soon I slow to turn into the driveway to the house. I'm not ready to break the contact of her holding onto me. Ren's fingers tighten on my abdominals.

"Can we go further?" She so closely echoes my thoughts it's as though her voice is in my head.

"Yeah." I gun the engine and ride out into the night.

It's late when we arrive home again, having ridden out of London into the leafy countryside. Ren sags as I remove her helmet and jacket, so I lift her off the bike and carry her—bridal style, how else?—inside, her head resting on my chest.

I linger in the bathroom, brushing my teeth and hoping I have the strength to not scare my bride with the force of my desire.

Whose idiot idea was it that we should share a bed?

Oh yeah, that was me.

The lights are low in my bedroom, and Ren is tucked up under the covers, eyes closed, breath even.

I remember the sight of her earlier, more beautiful than I could have dreamed. Her skin is creamy and smooth, her tits were made for being pressed together and sliding my cock between. Her waist is perfectly curved, and her long legs are begging for my kisses.

My cock springs to life as her words from this morning echo in my head.

Just an in-name-only marriage.

I want to jump on her and ravage her. Instead, I swallow, summon up the patience of some god I didn't think existed, and slip into bed, turning out the light.

It's been a stupidly long day. We're both exhausted.

I wonder if I'll be able to fall asleep with her here? I don't feel like I should, but she's the same tranquillity as the motorcycle, but more so.

I'm careful not to touch her, but lying in the dark, there's a rustle of fabric.

Ren's fingertips touch my abs, stroking the trail of hair that leads down.

Oh god, I want to let this happen, whatever this is.

"Ren?" I say softly. Putting my hand over hers, I feel the pulse there, fast.

"I thought since we're married...?"

My stomach gets heavy, even as my cock can't help but respond. Ren touching me is everything I've ever wanted. Well, that and my fake-wife's love. But she's only offering out of marital duty, and that's a hard no.

"You don't owe me anything." My voice is gruff. Dismissive.

"I do. I owe you a lot. Plus, I don't want anyone to suspect this isn't real, and I'm..." She gulps. "A virgin."

I wish she hadn't told me that. I don't know how it's possible, but I want her even more now than I did before. I'd be the first and only to claim my wife. Mine would be the first cock she came on. My hands would wipe away that smear of virgin blood and kiss any tears. And most of all, if we consummated this marriage, we'd have children.

I want that so much my heart might crack. I think it already did, the first time we met. A lightning strike that broke me open.

"You're curious?"

"Yeah." I hear her shrug, as though it's a matter of indifference whether it's me she's married to, or someone else.

I shift our hands up my chest before I can think, away from my throbbing cock and as though to stop the bleeding from my heart, the pain is that intense.

"Go to sleep, Ren."

She doesn't reply.

There's only the sound of our breathing. I'm glad of the dark so she can't see the longing in my face.

Minutes tick by. I'm not sleeping, and neither is she.

"Jasper?"

"Yes, princess?"

"What if someone sees us in bed together? And we're not even touching?"

I open my mouth to point out that's not going to happen. But she's scared of being caught in a lie, so logic won't soothe that fear.

I will murder whoever suggested a fake marriage. No donuts for past-Jasper. None. Sadistic prick.

"Will you hold me?" she asks in a small voice.

I groan inwardly as I make the only possible response. I gather her into my arms, careful to keep my rock-solid length away from her pert little arse. I'm a fool. Where any other man would either take what she's offering, or refuse her altogether, I'm going to do the worst of both worlds.

Because it's what's right for her. A warm embrace, and none of my needs met.

She's stiff as a board. My poor girl. Only last night she was being threatened by another mafia. Then discovering her older boss is her stalker, and that she just married him. It's a lot.

Not unreasonable that she might need comfort to fall asleep.

I softly stroke her hair and murmur, apparently

without volition. "It's okay. You're okay. My good girl. My sweet girl. You're okay."

And somehow every time my hand gets to her nape, she takes another breath.

My movements slow further, and eventually, I still at the bottom of the caress. At her throat. A possessive, controlling place. I could cut off her air. Her pulse beats under my thumb.

And she calms.

"That helps, huh?" I whisper.

She doesn't speak, but manages a tiny nod.

I leave my hand lightly clasped over her neck, and the tension ebbs from her.

"Ren." I say her name like it's a prayer. "I'm here. They're never going to take you away. I'll protect you from anything. I swear."

The darkness is a blanket that wraps us up together, away from our real-life selves as well as the harsh reality of day.

Her body softens. Relaxes with my hand over her throat. A claim, a promise. I might be a monster who could steal her life right now, but I am *her* monster, and I'm possessive. I won't give her up to anyone else. Her breathing evens out.

She's asleep.

And relief is the last thing I remember before I, too, fall into black.

7

REN

I wake in the dark. Three things strike me like flares of light.

First, I'm in Jasper's arms. His bicep is under my neck, his other arm over my shoulder and his hand clasping around, completing the necklace.

I've never felt so safe. I'm his collared pet, warm and snug and protected. Most people would be scared, I suppose, to discover they were married to their stalker. But knowing Jasper was looking after me all this time only makes me happier. This might only be six months, but I'm certain he'll care for me so long as we have this fake marriage.

Second: Jasper was stalking me. He's cared for me and yeah, I'm not thrilled he was watching me in my kitchen—I really hope I didn't do anything stupid while he was looking—that isn't a normal level of surveillance, even for a mafia employee. "Why do you think?", he replied earlier. And while my heart lifted, I didn't dare answer truthfully. That maybe he cares for me. To protect me, yes. But there's only one kingpin of Fulham, and he was outside *my* apartment. No one else's. I think I'm special to him.

Well, I thought so until he tucked me into bed rather than taking up my offer of being his real wife.

Third: this is my wedding night. And while I can't say that I'm unsatisfied—how could I be when Jasper licked me until I begged for mercy earlier on his desk—I'm still a virgin. Even though he made me come on his tongue, his fingers in my pussy, I need more.

And yes, I love this sweet, restrained version of Jasper, just holding me. But I know there's another side of him that I could awaken. I saw it in his office. I want more of that.

It could be minutes or hours since I fell asleep, but I'm awake now. As I lie in the dark, his hand a secure collar over my neck, the thought floats into my mind. Again.

A baby.

I want Jasper's baby.

No one could doubt our marriage if I had a baby.

And yeah, that's a good excuse. Another is that I want a part of him to remember this charmed, sweet time with him by. But I also want the sex that would get me pregnant, and yes, I'd hurt so badly leaving, but he's made it clear he doesn't want me permanently. Otherwise, why didn't he take me up on my offer when he joined me in bed?

I could give him my virginity as a gift.

Maybe he wouldn't even fully wake up, and act on instinct? Perhaps he'd think he was dreaming, and take me like he would any woman in his bed? And in a few months, before I was showing, I could move on. I'll never have him, but I'd have his child as well as the delicious memory of him inside me.

Is this a morally right thing to do? Definitely not. Without a doubt, it's death not donuts.

But I'm desperate. I need Jasper so much. I'm aching and empty, and I saw his erection earlier.

He's a man, and all the stereotypes say men constantly want sex. And even if maybe that's true for some men, it can't be correct for all, and for sure Jasper is not like most men. He's got more honour in his little finger than anyone I've ever met.

Which makes what I'm doing all the more reprehensible.

I'm just longing to touch my husband's dick, and definitely a bad person. But I'm so high after today, when he made all my dreams come true except the most important one, that I don't care.

I subtly wriggle backwards over the sheets. His hand is still at my neck, so secure. A bit further, moving slowly so I don't wake him, and then... I sigh with relief when my butt touches his hard length. His body wants me, at least.

Reaching behind, I oh-so-gently grasp the waistband of his soft cotton boxers, and slide it down. Then we're skin to skin, and it's indescribable how good it feels. He's hot and silky. Heated velvet stone as I lift my upper leg and rest it on his thigh, opening myself up.

I'm wet. My nipples are tingling. My clit pulses as I shift until... Ummph. I stuff my fist into my mouth to hold back a whimper. The head of his dick rests in my soaking folds. He's so solid. And *big*. Far bigger than I anticipated. Excitement flickers through me.

Though the logistics are turning out to be more difficult than I thought.

Shifting on the sheets, I'm scared to move too much in case I wake him. Yes, it's only the tip, and his dick feels amazing. But he's nowhere near where he needs to be. And how am I going to move enough to get him to come inside me?

Just the tip.

A sob of frustration wells up.

I can't do this.

Literally, he's too big, I don't think he'll fit. But also, what if he woke? Jasper would be so furious. I'd never want him to be as cross as he would be if he discovered what I was doing. I go to shift away, back to my side of the bed.

His hand tightens infinitesimally on my neck, cutting off my air for the time between heartbeats.

"Ren," comes a throaty growl.

I freeze.

"What are you doing?"

Then he slips his palm down, clasping my shoulder. It's ownership, that movement.

A whimper escapes me, and I arch into his touch. I

am helpless in my desire for this man. I love him excessively. His closeness feeds my soul, even when I'm trembling. What is my dangerous mafia boss husband going to do about me trying to ride his cock without his say-so?

He squeezes my hip, hard enough to bruise. Oh I hope it does. I'd wear his marks with pride.

"I asked you a question, *wife*, what are you doing?"

The tip of his cock is still pressed into my folds. Not fully inside, but neither of us has pulled away.

I think it's obvious what I'm trying to do. I'm attempting to get his cock into my pussy.

"Oops?" I say the first thing that pops into my head. "I slipped?"

His chest shakes with silent laughter.

"Try again." And his voice is laced with amused disbelief. He rolls his hips the smallest amount.

"Uh?" His slight movement has destroyed me. It sends sparks of pleasure from my core to my toes.

"Tell me, *wife*."

"I want a baby," I confess, beyond caring that my cheeks flame with humiliation. I'm caught. I might as well speak the truth. "I want you to give me a baby."

"My baby?"

I nod.

He shifts, still clasping my neck with that possessive tenderness, then his breath is at my temple.

"You want me to breed you, Ren?" His thumb brushes my cheek, and his other arm drags down over my belly, all the way to my mons. Then lower, sliding into the soft, slick place where his rigid shaft is at my entrance.

"Yes. Please." I don't care that I'm begging. I need him so much.

He explores my slippery folds before spiralling his fingertips towards my clit. And oooohhhh, my mind goes blank at the amazing sensation of him touching me inside and out.

"You're wet here again, princess," he rumbles into my ear. "Are you in heat, like a cat? I bet you're ready, aren't you? Fertile and needy."

"Breed me, husband." I have no idea why this is making me so hot, but I'm dripping. Creaming. I'm so aroused from him saying this and from my request.

"You want *my* baby? I'll give you all the seed for a baby. I'll fill you up. I'll make it overflow and pour out of you."

There's a pinch as he pushes against that barrier, and it hurts so good. His fingers relentlessly circle over my clit.

"When you've come again, this time on my cock. Then I'll pump into you, making you pregnant."

A sound of pure unadulterated need escapes my throat as he slowly, slowly fills me with his dick.

"That's it, take my whole length," he whispers into my ear. I writhe, but he's got me held between his cock spearing me, his arm over my ribcage and his hand at my breasts, and the other under my waist and his fingers on my clit.

There's a noise from my throat that might be a plea

for more, or a gasp that this is too much. He's huge. Jasper's massive dick is splitting me open.

"Uh-uh, you asked for it, princess. I'm going to give you exactly what you need. I'm going to fill you to overflowing."

He thrusts harder and deeper, and his fingers don't let up. I'm being owned by my alpha male husband. I wanted his dick? I have it. He's enormous and I can't get enough.

It's an onslaught I have no hope of resisting as he works me completely open. Even dusted with that hint of pain from him being so big, every slide of his body into mine causes sparks that fly up and down my spine. I grip his wrist, clasping it to me as he rolls my nipple.

"My filthy princess, aren't you? You're being such a good girl for me."

I'm just a puddle of girl. I'm his sheath. I don't think I have a brain anymore. I'm a spiralling bunch of cells with an urge to reproduce and hunger for pleasure.

"I'll give you a baby if you come again," he coaxes me.

I nod, unable to form even a three-letter word and the tension spirals higher and higher.

"So responsive and your little pussy is as incredible on my cock as it was to taste. I can't hold back much longer."

I cry out. My body isn't my own. When he said I was his, he wasn't joking. I belong to my husband now. The feeling is better than anything, and yet not quite enough.

"Come all over my cock." This time, he's not asking, he's ordering me in a low, raspy tone that, along with an adjustment to his angle inside me, sets off an explosion. I quake. I kick. I shudder as the orgasm tosses me around and squeezes pleasure from me I didn't know existed.

"My good girl. You're determined to make me come too, huh?" He sounds like his teeth are gritted.

The bliss still wracks through my limbs, and he strokes my belly proprietorially as he continues to pound into me.

"You're meant to carry my baby."

"Yes." I can't believe this.

As my orgasm fades away, my body is singing, buzzing in the aftermath. There's a sense of unreality because this is so exactly what I've always wanted. If this is a dream...

I reach back, needing to touch him too, finding his hip and the tense muscles of his bottom. I dig my fingers in, urging him silently on.

"You're so tight." He speeds up, and though I started this, he's using me for both our pleasure. Lying on my side, I can't do anything but take what he's giving me from behind. That sounds impersonal, but the dark, the covers, the warmth of his body, his arms braced around me, and the heat of his breath on my neck all mean this is intimate beyond my wildest dreams.

Being his receptacle is pure joy.

"My beautiful wife. My love."

And similarly to his dick penetrating me deeper than I realised was possible, given how big he is, his words have gone into my mind, despite my best efforts. They're in my head, as drugging as his touch.

"I'm going to love watching you with our baby. Holding your hand when you give birth the first, second, third, sixth, seventh time. I can't wait to do this again to be sure you're pregnant."

It's almost too much. The delicious stretch from his body in mine and his clever fingers, yes, but the future he's telling me about is even more seductive.

"You'd better get used to me, wife. When I fill you, I'm going to stay inside. You're mine, now."

People say all sorts of things they don't mean during sex, mindless with the animalistic urges that are at the fore. That's what the internet says, anyway. Don't trust anything a man says when his dick is hard.

But I want to believe Jasper. I can't, I shouldn't, I mustn't. I'll only trust him, get my hopes up, and in the morning, he'll let me down. And I don't care. If that's what happens, never mind. I'll have my kingpin's baby.

"You feel amazing. Perfect." He groans and his thrusts become slightly erratic, like he's losing control. "You were made to be loved by me."

I think that's what gives me the courage, or foolhardiness, to reveal what's been in my heart all along.

"I love you." I breathe the words. Almost silently. Jasper shouldn't hear above the muffled sounds of our bodies slapping together. He is supposed to be so intent on his shaft in my pussy that he doesn't notice. He's breeding me, after all. That's the new deal.

But he does. I'm sure he does, because he breaks at that moment. He shudders and holds me to him as wet heat floods into me.

His arms are tight over my chest, as he jerks, and his breath is hot and comforting on my ear. I've never felt so safe. He's not only around me, he's inside me. His big arms, his torso curled behind me. I couldn't escape, and I don't want to.

As his movements calm to stillness, he keeps me close like he can't bear to let me go. He doesn't pull out, keeping all his come plugged where it is needed—and oh so wanted.

I collapse further, boneless, held by him and speared on his dick.

Neither of us moves, and I think part of it is that there's an unspoken agreement that he's not releasing me, letting any of his seed spill, or even pulling out.

And he says into my hair, "I love you too."

8

JASPER

I awake to pounding on the bedroom door, and heaven.

Ren is cuddled into me, my little spoon. Her blonde hair spills over the pillow and her back is snug against my front. My morning wood is pressed to her bottom.

Wait. I frown. I was inside her when we fell asleep, plugging her, filling her. Reaching around, I cup her pussy. *My* pussy, because *she's mine*, now. It's sticky with our combined juices, and a satisfied smile tugs at my mouth.

Good.

I'll add to that. Fill her up again and again. I want her pregnant, and if that means keeping my seed in her that's an extra bonus.

The banging on the door sounds anew, and Ren stirs.

"Good morning, princess." I nuzzle the soft skin of her neck and remember how she begged me to breed her, and how she wanted my hand around her throat last night. My balls pull up and my cock hardens further.

"Mr Booth, it's Harvey."

"Jasper." She arches into me, and I groan as we notch together.

A flurry of knocks.

"You have to go to the door," Ren murmurs.

"Mr Booth! The man didn't turn up at Mrs Booth's apartment last night."

I let out a growl, bite her shoulder making her gasp, and roll out of bed.

I stride through the apartment and yank open the front door. "I told you to tell everyone to fuck off."

My second-in-command looks sheepish. "I know. I'm sorry. But I think we've got our blackmailer. The head of Battersea mafia is here. He said if you didn't see him, he'd have Mrs Booth deported."

"Battersea is behind this? Upstart little shit."

Harvey nods. Battersea is new money. Just old enough not to be modern, but not sufficiently old to have class. He's a crass idiot.

"We should have found him first. And he can't do that to Ren."

Harvey looks at me with that eloquent expression that says, *Yes, I know you get precisely what you want most of the time, but there are some things you cannot control, boss.*

I swear.

"I showed him into the reception room downstairs."

"You did the right thing," I grudgingly acknowledge, and close the door in Harvey's face. I can almost hear his sigh of exasperation as I walk away.

Back in the bedroom, Ren looks up at me with her soft blue eyes as wide as dinner plates and her hair tousled. By my hands, last night. She's naked, but has pulled the covers up to her chin, as though she could sneak underneath and disappear.

"They've come for me," she says in a tiny voice.

"Yep." While the temptation to get right back into that bed and rut her into the mattress again is almost unbearable, I don't. Vanquishing our foes first. More baby-making second. "We're going to face them. Together."

I pull open our wardrobe and there's a glow of satisfaction as I see all her new clothes hung next to my suits. I dress as usual. Perfunctory. Quick even, a necktie and a jacket, neat cufflinks.

"What should I wear?"

She regards the clothes doubtfully, her eyebrows pinched. She's slipped on a matching set of lacy white underwear and looks delectable. Good enough to eat.

So far as I'm concerned, her leggings and T-shirt are perfect. But something else is needed right now to feel confident as my princess.

"That one." It's a soft blue like her eyes, floor length, and has layers of sheer fabric.

"But…"

I unhook it from the hanger and shake it out, raising my eyebrows when she hesitates.

"I haven't even showered," she grumbles as she steps into the dress and I slide it up her body, pull up the zip and caressing the dip of her spine as I do.

"Good, then you'll smell freshly fucked by your husband."

She lets out a quiet sound of embarrassment and arousal, and I nudge her to support herself on the chest of drawers as I sort through the shoes under all her new dresses. I find a pair that are obscenely sexy. Straps, a high heel. I'd like to see Ren in these and nothing else. Instead, I kneel at her feet and drag her skirt up, caressing her calf.

"Lift."

She does as I say, and I slide the shoe into place. She wobbles a bit in one heel, grasping my shoulder as I put the other one on then allow her skirt to drop.

Guiding her to the mirror, I stand behind her, and admire my wife. *Mine*.

"Mrs Booth." Her cheeks pinken as I call her that. "You look beautiful."

Her hair is mussed from our night together, but that simply adds to her sexiness, even though the dress is relatively modest.

"Ready?"

She nods, and while I'd like to address the uncertainty in her expression, we have to deal with Battersea first.

By the time we're downstairs, outside the door to the reception room where Battersea is waiting, she's shaking. I smooth my hands over her shoulders and kiss her forehead. It's tempting to say things, make promises. But I've already told her. What she needs is proof.

That I love her. That I'll do anything—risk a mafia

war at very least—to keep her by my side. This might have begun as a marriage of convenience, but last night, I meant every word.

Battersea is lounging in a chair when we enter the room, tapping his fingers in what he must think is an intimidating show of power. It works on Ren, who blanches.

"Battersea."

"Why don't you send your men away, Fulham?" he drawls. "We both know you're part of that silly little London mafia club that pinky promises not to hurt anyone and I gave up my weapons at the door. We can settle this in a civilised manner."

I guide Ren to a sofa and sit, wrapping my arm around her shoulders and tucking her in close. Then I nod to my men, who have been keeping guard. Battersea has just revealed he knows nothing about me, or the London Mafia Syndicate.

"You didn't turn up for our appointment yesterday, Miss Smith—"

"Mrs Booth," I correct him.

Battersea smiles unpleasantly. "A sort of theft, marriage. I would have preferred not to involve you, Fulham. But be assured, this changes nothing."

"My wife won't be paying you anything, and I invite you to leave."

I should get a treat for being so calm and reasonable when I want to rip Battersea's throat out. Honestly, I might take that reward in the form of fucking Ren on this sofa as soon as possible.

"You still have two choices. Payment or deportation. What makes you think that a sham marriage will protect you?" Battersea scoffs, looking at Ren. "You could be prosecuted for falsely attempting to procure citizenship. This won't work."

He really is underestimating me. Fascinating. Perhaps I should throw my weight around in London a bit more. I've been too measured, clearly.

"I suppose he hasn't got even a million to spare, and has married you instead."

I feel Ren's head turn and look down. Our gazes meet and her expression is quizzical. Because she knows a million would be cheap compared to what yesterday cost.

She hasn't yet understood that marrying her could have cost ten billion, and I'd have found the money because to me, she's priceless.

"I bet he doesn't know anything about you," Battersea continues condescendingly. "Your favourite food, for instance."

"Donuts." We both speak simultaneously.

"Well done." He sneers. "You've been practising. That's not evidence in court."

"Our baby will be," Ren replies.

Battersea looks disconcerted for a second. Ren bites her lip, but the corners of her mouth turn up as she smooths her palm over her perfectly flat belly.

"That baby will have dark hair and green eyes." I know it. I'm certain. And if they don't? Never mind, I'll keep breeding my girl until we have a baby who is my mirror image.

"That will be irrelevant to the detention centre staff." Battersea shrugs. "Unless you pay up."

And that's when my patience snaps. I'm across the room and have the arsehole held by the throat in a second. His feet are off the ground.

"Nobody threatens *my wife*." I'm so furious, my voice is hardly recognizable.

"You bastard." Battersea struggles impotently, going red in the face. "Let me go! Westminster will kill you for this!"

"I went to school with Westminster," I reply. "He *loves* his wife. I have no idea why you imagine his sense of fair play would preclude me from protecting mine."

Battersea stills, and I think finally recognises that he's in a terrible situation of his own making. "Just a hundred thousand then."

I snort with laughter. Amazingly, he still thinks he has power in this situation.

"We haven't played death or donuts yet today, Mrs Booth." I'd like nothing more than to unleash my men on this piece of shit and let all their most savage instincts run riot. But apparently I haven't been providing enough evidence of my own ruthlessness, so I don't call anyone in.

"I suppose we haven't," she replies, a tremor in her voice.

"What's your verdict on a man who attempted to extort money from a vulnerable young woman? And abuse his position of authority."

"Did he have to?" she asks. So fair, my wife. So thorough. I love that about her.

"No." I grimace. "He's rich enough."

"That doesn't sound like he needs donuts."

"Your decision, princess?" I'm running out of composure. Battersea thrashes at a weird angle, scrabbling at my hand, trying to get me to release him. "Donuts, or..."

I turn to Ren. Her expression darkens and her chin juts out a little. I'm smiling before she's even said the word.

"Death."

"No donuts for you."

"Gun!" Ren shouts as I feel him manage to get his hand to his ankle and pull out a weapon. But I'm faster, and I have a fuck of lot more to live for. Wrenching the thing from his grasp, I toss it away.

My other hand goes to Battersea's temple, and I yank. His neck snaps instantly.

I drop his lifeless body to the floor and turn to Ren, taking two steps before I'm stopped short by her expression.

Pure fear. Absolute terror.

I've wrecked everything, I've revealed the horror of my true self—

She barrels into me, and for a second, I'm too surprised to do anything. Then I hear it.

"Jasper. Oh Jasper." She's sobbing. "I was so scared I'd lose you when I saw him pull that gun. Thank god you're safe. I love you so much."

My arms wrap around her, bracketing her and keeping her close. But it's not necessary. She's clinging to me, and my heart is expanding. There is no limit to how much I love my wife.

She's relieved, and so am I. I hold her tighter still. I could have lost her. A glance across the room reveals the gun Battersea pulled from a holster on his ankle. Printed plastic. No metal, that must be how it got through my men's checks.

"I know we said six months, but oh god please—"

"Forever. I told you. You're mine, now."

Hope dawns on her face as she peeks up. "Really?"

"You always were. I love you with every fibre of my being, Ren."

"Not just an in-name-only thing?" she checks.

"I've been inside you. I claimed you. If you wanted my cock, the price was complete ownership. Permanently. No half measures. No faking." I should have told her this yesterday. I have to have this woman. I need to own her, body, heart, and soul.

She burrows her face into my shirt, holding on. Breathing in unevenly, she shudders out the last words I'm expecting. "Thank you."

I slide my fingers into her hair and gently tug until her head falls back. "Not, 'you promised me a marriage of convenience'?"

"No." Her grin lights her up. "I always wanted you, too."

"Right." I hoist her by her bottom, into my arms and

she hooks her hands around my nape, pressing herself to me.

"Where are we going?" she asks as we get to the stairs.

"Back to our bed, to finish what we started last night." I feel rather than hear her delighted giggle. "Getting you pregnant."

EPILOGUE
JASPER

10 YEARS LATER

You'd think that having eight children would dull the novelty, but no. Not even slightly. I hear the stomping of small feet on the stairs then down the hallway, and smile.

My office is hardly a bastion of solitude and quiet anymore. Leather-bound books and fountain pens have given way to board books and crayons. I love it.

It used to be that people were unalived for interrupting me. But the kids?

Ren told me very firmly that they always get donuts, never death.

"Daddy, where are my socks?"

I look up as our eldest child, Justine, bursts through the door.

"In your sock drawer, little one?" I quirk an eyebrow up.

Her mouth goes into a flat line. "You're so basic. I've looked there."

"It is a good place to find socks."

"I mean my *pink* socks." She scowls, looking particularly adorable.

"Come here."

For such a small creature barefoot on a deep carpet, Justine is astonishingly noisy. It's sweet really. Our youngest daughter, Marie, is a mouse. More similar to Ren.

Justine huffs as I scoot my chair back and tap my knees. But she knows the deal, sitting across my lap and accepting her cuddle with all the grace of a disgruntled badger.

One day, Justine will help me with the Fulham mafia. Maybe she'll take it over. I like that idea. She's feisty, our first-born. She'll understand the death-or-donuts game, I'm certain.

"Daddeeeeey," Justine complains when my hug goes on for too long. By which she means, more than three seconds.

I sigh. There are only two ways to get a decent cuddle around here, and neither my wife nor our newborn baby are in this room. "Alright, let's search for these socks."

Justine scrambles off my lap and gallops out of the office like a miniature hippo, and I follow behind. We've made some adjustments since starting our family. One of those is that our apartment now encompasses the floor that used to be my office, meaning the kids can come and get me anytime I'm working on day-to-day stuff. If I'm downstairs in one of the reception rooms, that's where they're strictly banned.

No death for the babies. Not even seeing threats of it. I don't forget that rule.

Probably I ought to sort through the washing basket or something, but I head for the lounge, where there are giggles and shouts. Unlike our eldest daughter, I can be stealthy. I pause in the doorway.

Ren is sitting on the floor, our youngest son in a sling, crashed out on her chest. She's leaning against the sofa, and our two toddlers are in baskets, also fast asleep. Elodie, Clement, Lucas, and Delphine are gathered around a board game, focussed intently.

"Are you sure that's within the rules?" Lucas, our eldest boy, says. He's seven, and as serious as Justine is bright. He loves rules. I think he'll be horrified when he's older and knows how flexible I am with the law.

"'Tis so," replies Elodie.

Watching them, all healthy and happy and squabbling makes my chest ache with contentment.

My gaze flicks back to Ren as she leans on the squishy edge of the sofa. A glimpse of Ren's belly, and my cock stirs.

My wife is five months pregnant, and as ripe, sweet, and perfect as a late summer plum. She's curvier than when we met, and I adore her even more. There's no limit to my love for her, and my family.

As though she feels my regard, Ren looks over. Our

gazes meet, and I lazily drag mine down her body, then up to her eyes, making my thoughts very clear.

Both of us find Ren being pregnant—and my breeding her—the ultimate aphrodisiac.

"I love you," I mouth.

"I love you, too," she mouths back.

"And I'm going to breed you," I add silently.

Her grin is positively wicked.

"Daddy!" Justine's cry sounds behind me. "Did you find my socks?"

EXTENDED EPILOGUE
JASPER

10 YEARS ON, THE NEXT MORNING

The mornings are still for us. Thankfully the kids haven't inherited my insomnia, and mostly, I use the time when I'm up before the sun rises to wake Ren in the most delicious way. Licking her until she screams.

But sometimes she looks so sweet and sleepy, peaceful, that I don't wake her when my brain is buzzing at four-thirty. Today, I just kissed her mouth and stroked her cheek. I had my fill of her last night. Or rather, I filled her up.

I still love falling asleep with my cock inside her, keeping all that sperm where it's needed. It's an ownership instinct, I suppose. I bred her, she's mine.

I'm down in my office, going through some numbers when there's a gentle knock on the door and my wife slips in.

"Good morning." I indulge in looking at her, leaning

back in my chair. She's wearing her sleep T-shirt, but her legs and feet are bare.

"Mr Booth." She casts her gaze down. "I have a favour to ask you for."

My eyebrows raise. I very nearly just outright say, that's fine. Whatever she wants, I want.

"Hmm." I make my tone severe. "What's your request, princess?"

"Please... I'd like to take the children on vacation to Hawaii."

"Hawaii?" I didn't realise she wanted to go there. Probably one of the kids has set their heart on it. But this is much more fun as a game. And it is a game, I'm certain of that as Ren toys with the hem of her T-shirt, pulling it up to reveal the tops of her thighs. She's very obviously pregnant and it makes her even sexier. "That's going to be expensive, don't you think? When did you want to go?"

"Before the baby is born?"

Next week would be ideal. We'll book it today.

"Please? I'll do *anything*." She meets my gaze, and her eyes go big and innocent.

I palm my cock, which has gone hard with the inevitability of sunrise.

"You'll have to earn it, princess."

"Of course. I'm willing to work." Her nod is far too eager, and I know what she wants.

"Come here and suck my cock, and we'll see about those plane tickets. If you're good enough, I'll pay for it all."

We exchange a secret smile, almost hiding it from the personas we're taking on.

She's at my feet in a few quick steps, stripping off her T-shirt to reveal that gorgeously curved body, her tits already larger in anticipation of our new child. Then she kneels...

I should act cool, but fuck that. I strip my flies open and free my erection.

My wife puts her mouth over the tip.

I groan. So good.

She eases down and down, into her throat. The pleasure is instant.

"That's it. Take it." I flex my hips and she hums.

There's nothing better for either of us than making the other feel good. Sure, we share a breeding kink. That's our thing, and I'll be breeding Ren forever, even when we don't actually have any more children, which isn't far off. I'm thinking ten is a great place to stop and then I'll get the snip. And continue playing our breeding game, filling her up and knowing we can sleep through the night without any babies waking us.

Breeding her and bringing up our kids is who we are. It's a way of being. We understand each other through our family and our mutual need.

But the give and take is pure love. It's telling each other that we're always more than parents. We're more than the Fulham mafia.

Most of all, we're never alone. Through the hardest decisions and the gut-wrenching moments of life, Ren and I always have time to please each other.

So yeah, I don't feel bad when the head of my cock hits the back of her throat. Or for the savage moan that escapes me. Not even for the way I take her hair and wrap all that silk around my fist and force her deeper.

I know she loves doing this for me as much as I adore eating her delicious pussy.

She does something with her tongue—it's a trick she's done on me before, but I'm always too far gone to analyse what it is.

"Ren, princess. Love. Oh god. I need..."

She's shifting before I am, allowing me to stand so I can control this. Sitting on her heels she opens her throat.

Letting out a feral growl, I fuck her mouth. After years and years, I don't have to hold back. We both know how this is. I can feel her limits as easily as I can feel my own pleasure.

Her eyes water and I tighten my grip on her hair, forcing myself further because it feels fucking perfect.

My balls tingle and tighten up. And while Ren loves it when I come down her throat, or over her belly, or in her pussy, or frankly anywhere that involves her, I must take advantage of this moment of privacy and calm in my office.

"Enough." I pull out of her mouth with a wet pop. Saliva dribbles down her chin as she looks up at me, dazed.

"I have to fuck you. Get over the desk."

She scrambles to obey, hasty as if there was her livelihood on the line. Though she's just eager.

"Come slut," I murmur as I drag my gaze over her

bent over my desk, knees already apart, beautiful belly hanging down. Her pussy is glistening.

"Yes, Mr Booth."

Grasping her arse, I kneed and stroke it. Then I land a hard slap on one cheek. She cries out and the mark goes deliciously pink.

"Thank you," she whispers.

I smack her again, harder. Then a few more times just to sensitise her. A reminder that she's mine, first and foremost.

"You're my favourite breeding toy, aren't you?"

"Yes," she whines, and drags her hands over the desk, tipping several piles of papers onto the floor.

That'll get her more of a spanking later, across my knee. But right now, I need to be inside her. A second to notch at her entrance and enjoy the anticipation, then I thrust, and she groans.

"You feel huge." She pushes herself onto my cock as I ease into a rhythm. "Even bigger between my legs than in my mouth."

"You're so tight. My perfect little whore."

"I know, I know. You break me open every time."

I have both hands on her hips now, slamming into her. We're both panting. I'm almost cross-eyed. Her back is so lovely, and her arse is squishy and peachy pink from being slapped. Ripe.

"Come for me, Ren."

She nods, arching her spine and spreading her legs to get more contact between us.

Very occasionally she can come without me stroking

her clit, and fuck that is a privilege like no other. But so is coaxing her orgasms out of her with my hands and cock and tongue.

She keens, and there are a few seconds where I'm hanging on by a thread.

"Do you need...?"

I can barely think. My balls have pulled up. I'm ready to explode into her.

"No, I..." My wife shudders and grips me like a vice as she comes on my cock without a touch to her clit at all.

The connection is instant. She triggers my orgasm and I'm spilling into her in ream after ream that wreck me. I unload every drop of semen in my balls. I swear I empty my whole soul every time my princess makes me come.

I collapse onto one forearm over her, kissing down her spine and over her shoulders.

"I love you." I say it over and over, between kisses, while still inside her. Always keeping her filled with my cock and come. Overflowing, yes, but holding in as much as possible.

"I love you so much. You're everything to me you know that, right?" she whispers back, like it's our secret.

"I know." I stroke her belly. "My wife. I love you."

THANKS

Thank you for reading, I hope you enjoyed it.

Want to read a little more Happily Ever After? Click to get exclusive epilogues and free stories! or head to EvieRoseAuthor.com

If you have a moment, I'd really appreciate a review wherever you like to talk about books. Reviews, however brief, help readers find stories they'll love.

Love to get the news first? Follow me on your favored social media platform - I love to chat to readers and you get all the latest gossip.

If the newsletter is too much like commitment, I recommend following me on BookBub, where you'll just get new release notifications and deals.

- amazon.com/author/evierose
- bookbub.com/authors/evie-rose
- instagram.com/evieroseauthor
- tiktok.com/@EvieRoseAuthor

INSTALOVE BY EVIE ROSE

Accidentally Kidnapping the Mafia Boss

I might have kidnapped him, but the mafia boss isn't going to let me go.

Grumpy Bosses

Older Hotter Grumpier

My billionaire boss catches me reading when I should be working. And the punishment...?

Tall, Dark, and Grumpy

When my boss comes to fetch me from a bar, I'm expecting him to go nuts that I'm drunk and described my fake boyfriend just like him. But he demands marriage...

Silver Fox Grump

He was my teacher, and my first off-limits crush. Now he's my stalker, and my boss.

Stalker Kingpins

Spoiled by my Stalker

From the moment we lock eyes, I'm his lucky girl... But there's a price to pay

Kingpin's Baby

I beg the Kingpin for help... And he offers marriage.

Owned by her Enemy

I didn't expect the ruthless new kingpin—an older man, gorgeous and hard—to extract such a price for a ceasefire: an arranged marriage.

His Public Claim

My first time is sold to my brother's best friend

Pregnant by the Mafia Boss

Baby Proposal

My boss walked in on me buying "magic juice" online... And now he's demanding to be my baby's daddy!

Groom Gamble

I accidentally gave my hot boss my list of requirements for a perfect husband: tall, gray eyes, nice smile, big d*ck. High sperm count.

Kingpin's Nanny

My grumpy boss bought my whole evening as a camgirl!

London Mafia Bosses

Captured by the Mafia Boss

I might be an innocent runaway, but I'm at my friend's funeral to avenge her murder by the mafia boss: King.

Taken by the Kingpin

Tall, dark, older and dangerous, I shouldn't want him.

Stolen by the Mafia King

I didn't know he has been watching me all this time.

I had a plan to escape. Everything is going perfectly at my wedding rehearsal dinner until *he* turns up.

Caught by the Kingpin

The kingpin growls a warning that I shouldn't try his patience by attempting to escape.

There's no way I'm staying as his little prisoner.

Claimed by the Mobster

I'm in love with my ex-boyfriend's dad: a dangerous and powerful mafia boss twice my age.

Snatched by the Bratva

I have an excruciating crush on this man who comes into the coffee shop. Every day. He's older, gorgeous, perfectly dressed. He has a Russian accent and silver eyes.

Kidnapped by the Mafia Boss

I locked myself in the bathroom when my date pulled out a knife. Then a tall dark rescuer crashed through the door… and kidnapped me.

Held by the Bratva

"Who hurt you?"

Before I know it, my gorgeous neighbour has scooped me up into his arms and taken me to his penthouse. And he won't let me go.

Seized by the Mafia King

I'm kidnapped from my wedding

Abducted by the Mafia Don

"Touch her and die."

Filthy Scottish Kingpins

Forbidden Appeal

He's older and rich, and my teenage crush re-surfaces as I beg the former kingpin to help me escape a mafia arranged marriage. He stares at me like I'm a temptress he wants to banish, but we're snowed in at his Scottish castle.

Captive Desires

I was sent to kill him, but he's captured me, and I'm at his mercy. He says he'll let me go if I beg him to take his...

Eager Housewife

Her best friend's dad is advertising for a free use convenient housewife, and she's the perfect applicant.

CONTEMPORARY ROMANCE BY EVIE ROSE WRITING AS EVE PENDLE

Secrets of Wildbrook

Her Nemesis until 5pm

He's grumpy, she's sunshine. They're about to get snowed in together. And there's only one bed.

Her Fake Date Until Midnight

He's hot. Rich. Domineering. And grumpy.

She's kind, trapped, and soon to be broke.

Her Grumpy Neighbour until Halloween

He's gorgeous but grumpy

She's conspicuous, cheerful, and in a lot of trouble

Her Boss until Christmas

She can't stand him, but his offer is too tempting

He's a cynical billionaire with too many secrets

Printed in Dunstable, United Kingdom